STORM BRINGER

"At this hour
Lie at my mercy all mine enemies."

The Tempest, Act 4 Scene 1

Titles in Dark Reads:

Badger Publishing Limited, Oldmedow Road, Hardwick Industrial Estate, King's Lynn PE30 4JJ
Telephone: 01438 791037

www.badgerlearning.co.uk

TIM COLLINS

Illustrated by Amit Tayal

Storm Bringer ISBN 978-1-78464-437-6

Publisher: Susan Ross
Senior Editor: Danny Pearson
Editorial Coordinator: Claire Morgan
Copyeditor: Cheryl Lanyon
Designer: Bigtop Design Ltd
Illustrator: Amit Tayal

2 4 6 8 10 9 7 5 3 1

STORM BRINGER

Contents

CHAPTER 1
THE WIND

Fed up, Ariel looked at his map.

He had no idea how to get back to camp.

He just wanted this week to be over so he could go home.

He heard footsteps behind him. Sebastian was coming down the hill.

"Let me help you with that," said Sebastian.

He ripped the map out of Ariel's grasp and it blew away.

Ariel couldn't stop himself.

He raised his hands, pointed them at Sebastian and muttered under his breath.

A huge gust of wind swept down the hill and blew Sebastian off his feet. He tumbled over and struck his leg on a rock.

He grabbed his shin in pain.

Ariel grinned.

CHAPTER 2
CLIFF-HANGER

Ariel stood with his back to the cliff edge and gripped the rope.

"Tip your body back until your feet are flat against the rock," said Mr Patel. "Then let the rope slide through your hands and walk yourself down."

Ariel couldn't make himself do it. He knew it was safe, but his stomach jumped whenever he tried to lean over.

"I'll give you a hand," said Sebastian.

He stepped forwards and shoved Ariel in the chest.

Ariel slipped back and screamed. He fell a few feet, then the rope pulled tight and smacked him into the cliff face.

CHAPTER 3
THE STORM

Ariel looked up at the cliff. He'd made it safely down but his legs were still shaking.

Sebastian had looked over the edge and laughed the whole time.

Now he was coming down and it was time to get him back.

Ariel lifted his hands and murmured under his breath.

A strong wind ripped through the valley, whipping leaves and branches into a spiral.

The wind circled Sebastian and he swung
wildly on the rope.

He slammed into the rock again and again.
Ariel could hear him screaming above the
howling wind.

Ariel lowered his hands and the storm
died down.

CHAPTER 4
THE THREAT

"I know it was you," said Sebastian.

They were back at the campsite and Ariel was brushing his teeth in the shower block.

"I don't know what you mean," said Ariel.

He spat out a mouthful of toothpaste.

Ariel walked outside and Sebastian came after him.

"You caused the storms," said Sebastian. "I know you did it and when we get back I'm going to prove it to everyone."

Ariel felt like creating a whirlwind to rip Sebastian off his feet.

"You're a freak," said Sebastian. "And as soon as people find out they'll lock you up forever."

Ariel went back into his tent.

His heart pounded as he thought about what Sebastian had said. He'd managed to keep his powers secret his whole life. Now he'd risked everything.

If Sebastian could prove it, Ariel would never live a normal life again. He'd be trapped in a lab while scientists poked and prodded him.

He couldn't let that happen.

CHAPTER 5
THE TEMPEST

Ariel looked out at the waves. It was the final day of the trip and he was meant to be taking part in a windsurfing lesson.

Lots of pupils were already on the sea. Sebastian was furthest out.

Ariel needed to make sure no one would ever find out about his powers.

He could only think of one way.

Ariel would stir up another storm, his biggest one yet. A storm so powerful it would wash Sebastian out to sea and he'd never have to worry about him again.

He held his hands out and muttered under his breath.

A huge wave rose under Sebastian's board. Above it, thunder clapped and heavy rain started to pour...

STORY FACTS

This story was inspired by William Shakespeare's famous play *The Tempest*, which was written around 1611.

The Tempest features a character called Ariel who can cause storms. However, he does it to serve a magician called Prospero rather than for his own revenge.

In *The Tempest*, Ariel is a spirit of the air with magical powers. The actor playing him will often fly above the stage on a wire.

The Tempest also inspired a classic science fiction film called *Forbidden Planet*, which was made in 1956.

QUESTIONS

What does Sebastian take from Ariel?
(page 8)

Which part of his body does Sebastian hurt?
(page 10)

Who pushes Ariel off the cliff?
(page 14)

Why does Sebastian call Ariel a freak?
(page 22)

Why are the pupils out on the water?
(page 26)

Tim Collins has written over 50 books for children and adults, including *Wimpy Vampire*, *Cosmic Colin*, *Monstrous Maud* and *Dorkius Maximus*. His other teenage fiction for Badger Learning includes *The Black-Eyed Girl*, *Joke Shop* and *Mr Perfect*. Tim has won awards in the UK and Germany.

Amit Tayal was born and educated in India. From 5th Grade he used to trade superhero sketches for help with his homework. He started his career as an animator in Delhi and is now based in Reading. Amit likes to travel and loves console gaming.